Planet of the Pies
Cloudy With a Chance of Meatballs 3

Written by Judi Barrett

Drawn by Isidre Monés

Atheneum Books for Young Readers
New York London Toronto Sydney New Delhi

To Pelf and Pies
—J. B.

To my grandsons,
Marti and Gerard
—I. M.

ATHENEUM BOOKS FOR YOUNG READERS
An imprint of Simon & Schuster Children's Publishing Division
1230 Avenue of the Americas, New York, New York 10020
Text copyright © 2013 by Judi Barrett
Illustrations copyright © 2013 by Isidre Monés
ATHENEUM BOOKS FOR YOUNG READERS is a registered trademark of Simon & Schuster, Inc.
Atheneum logo is a trademark of Simon & Schuster, Inc.
For information about special discounts for bulk purchases, please contact Simon & Schuster Special Sales
at 1-866-506-1949 or business@simonandschuster.com.
The Simon & Schuster Speakers Bureau can bring authors to your live event. For more information
or to book an event, contact the Simon & Schuster Speakers Bureau at 1-866-248-3049 or visit our website
at www.simonspeakers.com.
Book design by Lauren Rille
The text for this book is set in ITC Cheltenham.
The illustrations for this book are rendered in pen and ink with watercolors.
Manufactured in China
0613 SCP
First Edition
10 9 8 7 6 5 4 3 2 1
Library of Congress Cataloging-in-Publication Data
Barrett, Judi.
Cloudy with a chance of meatballs 3 : planet of the pies / Judi Barrett. — 1st ed.
p. cm.
Summary: When astronauts land on Mars, their first discovery is a substance not unlike pie filling,
and Kate and Henry are eager to go taste some, but Grandpa, who may have some inside information,
discourages them.
ISBN 978-1-4424-9027-7
ISBN 978-1-4424-9028-4 (eBook)
[1. Life on other planets—Fiction. 2. Astronauts—Fiction. 3. Weather—Fiction. 4. Food—Fiction. 5. Mars—
Fiction.] I. Title. II. Title: Cloudy with a chance of meatballs three. III. Title: Planet of the pies.
PZ7.B2752Clp 2013
[E]—dc23   2012051345

It was Tuesday evening. We were watching TV with Grandpa. He picked up the newspaper and was shocked when he saw the front-page headline. He held it up to show us.

ASTRONAUTS LAND ON MARS. SPECULATION AS TO WHAT OR WHO THEY WILL FIND THERE.

Henry and I looked at each other in disbelief.

I asked Grandpa what he thought they'd find on Mars. Henry said he hoped it would be aliens. Grandpa said we'll have to wait and see, and if it's aliens, he hoped they'd be friendly ones.

Moments later a breaking-news alert appeared on the TV.

A noticeably startled reporter blurted out, "We interrupt this program for some earth-shaking news. We've just been informed that astronauts have discovered a thick, glutinous substance on Mars, both on the ground and falling from the sky. Here's a crazy thought: could it be pie filling? That'd be pretty weird. Stay tuned, and we'll have an exclusive, first-of-its-kind interview with our astronauts, live from Mars!"

Henry and I jumped up and down, yelling about how much we love pie and wondering why it can't rain pie here on Earth.

We told Grandpa we wanted to go to Mars for our vacation this summer. He said he didn't think that was possible, because it's a very long trip, we don't have a spaceship, and we're not astronauts.

Henry said he'd like to become an astronaut and fly to Mars in a spaceship, where he could eat lots of pie and meet aliens.

I said I'd be happy just eating pie here on Earth.

Grandpa reminded us that we have some pie in the fridge.

Henry reminded Grandpa that it wasn't Martian pie and wondered what *that* would taste like.

Grandpa said maybe we'd all get to find out someday, but enough about Mars and pie for now. It was time to go to bed.

We kissed Grandpa good night, he wished us sweet dreams, and we scampered upstairs.

Grandpa sat down to watch the rest of the breaking news.
Then he dozed off and dreamt about a most unusual place. . . .

. . . To my great surprise, I found myself on Mars, all suited up as Mission Commander, along with my crew of fellow astronauts. It had been a long, long ride, and we were glad to have finally landed safely. We climbed out of our spaceship cautiously and surveyed the landscape for any signs of life.

We could hardly believe our eyes. What we saw was *pie*. And lots of it. It was all over the place and even raining down from the sky.

Despite the adverse weather conditions, we set up our camera for TV transmission. Pie splattered onto the lens. It was also on our suits, our boots, and our helmets.

It tasted awfully good.

The TV interview was about to start. I wiped the pie off the lens. We looked pretty messy. And when we were asked what we had found so far, we all yelled out . . . "PIE!"

I thought, *First, it's meatballs in Chewandswallow, and now, it's pie on Mars.*

In the distance we saw a group of umbrella-carrying Martians coming toward us. There were tall ones and short ones and some with strange pets. They were all mumbling, "Xcrdfk kg sdlpw lhnwy."

The reporter asked about the approaching Martians and what they were saying. It was a peculiar-sounding language—lots of jumbled-up consonants. We were puzzled as to what they were trying to tell us, but they appeared to be friendly.

I listened carefully, and something about that peculiar sound rang a LOUD bell! I had taken Martian in high school, instead of Spanish or French. When I told this to my crew, they were amazed and relieved.

So were the Martians. They handed us a book titled *Martian into English in Twelve Hours or Less*. It really came in handy for my buddies!

The Martians said they'd been waiting for years for us to come and visit them. They had headed toward Earth several times, but they got scared at the last minute and flew right back to Mars.

Now here we were on Mars, and here they were with this annoying pie problem. It had started raining pie about six months ago, between 5 p.m. and 7 p.m., just in time for dessert.

They desperately needed help. It was just too much pie. They were stepping in it and dragging it into their homes on their feet, and their space cars got stuck in it.

This was definitely a huge problem and the last thing we thought we'd find on Mars. But we said we'd help them figure out a solution. And we did!

They took us on a tour in their double-decker space bus. They drove in and around the pie, pointing out their homes, schools, parks, Martian monuments, and natural wonders. We saw just how much pie had piled up on the ground. They had built walls, houses, mountains, and sculptures with it, but it was apparent they couldn't keep this up.

What they caught on their plates between five and seven, they ate for dessert. But the situation was most definitely getting out of hand.

The Martians prepared quite an unusual feast for us that first night. They even held a pie-eating contest for dessert.

And guess who won?

They put us up at the Mars Motel.

The next morning we all got together to discuss the pie problem. I'd been thinking about it all night and had come up with an idea! I suggested catching the pies, exporting them back to Earth in boxes, and selling them. We'd be partners in a pie business and would call it "Martian Pie—Tastes Out of This World."

They really liked that!
But how would we catch the pies?

I recommended constructing giant nets. The pies would land safely, and we could slide them off and put them in boxes. Everyone agreed that this was a wonderful idea and a fine solution to the pie problem.

And so our joint venture officially began.

MARTIAN PIE
TASTES OUT OF THIS WORLD

We brought samples of the pies back to Earth for scientific analysis to make sure they passed our safety codes . . . and they did!

So we packaged them and shipped them off everywhere. And I mean absolutely EVERYWHERE!

. . . Grandpa awoke from his dream the next morning to see more breaking news on the TV. The reporter said that the thick, glutinous substance that he thought *might* be pie filling was just wishful thinking on his part! It was, actually, unusually thick and colorful Martian rain. He apologized for the error.

The front-page headline read: "No Pie on Mars. Just Bad Weather." Under it was a picture of the astronauts.

Henry and I noticed the resemblance to Grandpa and asked him, "Is that you in the picture?"

"How could it be," he said. "I wasn't on Mars. I was asleep in my chair."

After dinner that evening, we all watched TV while Grandpa served us pie for dessert.

"I bet this tastes a lot better than Martian pie!" said Henry.

"I'll bet it does," said Grandpa proudly, "because I made it myself."